RAMADAN

HOLIDAY CELEBRATIONS

Kieran Walsh

Rourke

Publishing LLC

Vero Beach, Florida 32964

www.rourkepublishing.com

PHOTO CREDITS: © All photos Associated Press

Cover: *Muslim children enjoying a meal after sunset during Ramadan*

Editor: Frank Sloan

Cover Design by Nicola Stratford

Library of Congress Cataloging-in-Publication Data

Walsh, Kieran.
  Ramadan / Kieran Walsh.
     p. cm. — (Holiday celebrations)
Summary: Describes the traditions and festivities of the Muslim holiday Ramadan.
Includes bibliographical references and index.
  ISBN 1-58952-223-0 (hardcover)
  1. Ramadan—Juvenile literature. 2. °åld al-Fiòtr—Juvenile
literature. 3. Fasts and feasts—Islam—Juvenile literature. 4.
Islam—Rituals—Juvenile literature. [1. Ramadan. 2. Fasts and
feasts—Islam. 3. Holidays.] I. Title. II. Holiday celebrations (Vero
Beach, Fla.)
  BP186.4 .W35 2002
  297.3'62—dc21
                                                    2002003671

Printed in the USA

pc/pc

TABLE OF CONTENTS

THE NINTH MONTH

Ramadan (RAH mah DAHN) is the ninth month of the Islamic calendar. **Islam** is a religion based on the teachings of a book called the **Qur'an**. People who practice Islam are called **Muslims**. There are over a billion Muslims in the world. For Muslims, the month of Ramadan is a time of prayer and reflection. Ramadan usually takes place in the fall or winter. In 2002 it begins on November 6.

Girls take time to study the
Qur'an during Ramadan.

FASTING

During Ramadan, Muslims practice **Sawm**, or fasting. This means that Muslims do not eat or drink during the daylight hours of Ramadan. Fasting is an opportunity to remember the less fortunate and focus on **Allah**, the God of Islam. After sunset, Islamic families enjoy a meal called **Iftar**. Iftar usually involves **Hibiscus**, a kind of tea, and **Kunafa**, a sweet pastry.

Sweet pastries are prepared for Iftar.

FRIENDS AND FAMILY

Ramadan is also a time for friends and family. In the evenings after the traditional Iftar meal, people spend time with their relatives and neighbors. Muslims exchange cards and gifts. People wish each other "Ramadan **Mubarak**," which means "A Blessed Ramadan."

Muslim worshippers gather to eat and spend time together.

MOSQUES

A **mosque** is an Islamic house of worship. There are more than 1,200 mosques in the United States. During Ramadan Muslims spend much of their time in mosques. They recite prayers like the **Tarawih**, a special night prayer. Muslims also go to mosques during Ramadan to read and study the Qur'an.

An Islamic house of worship is called a mosque.

Sailors pray in a chapel aboard the U.S.S. Theodore Roosevelt.

A Muslim mother buys toys for her children during an Eid al-Fitr celebration.

THE NIGHT OF POWER

The last ten days of Ramadan are especially important to Muslims. The 27th night of Ramadan is known as the Night of Power. It is believed that on this night Allah delivered the Qur'an to a man named **Muhammad**. Muhammad was responsible for spreading the teachings of Islam through the world. Many Muslims spend this entire night in prayer.

Thousands of worshippers spend the 27th night of Ramadan in prayer.

EID AL-FITR

The next month after Ramadan is **Shawwal**. On the first three days of Shawwal, Muslims celebrate **Eid al-Fitr**, meaning "the Festival of Breaking the Fast." For Eid al-Fitr, Muslims gather together for large meals. People dress in their finest clothes and decorate their homes in lights. Everyone shares hugs and handshakes.

Eid al-Fitr is a time of celebration.

FESTIVALS

In many of the Muslim countries around the world, special Eid al-Fitr festivals are held. Celebrations for Eid al-Fitr are also becoming popular in the western world. In December 2000, about 4,000 Muslims held an Eid al-Fitr festival in Ottawa, Canada. This festival included a variety of delicious foods to eat and games for Muslim children.

Children enjoy an Eid al-Fitr festival.

RAMADAN AT THE WHITE HOUSE

On November 19, 2001, President George Bush and First Lady Laura Bush held an Iftar at the White House. This was the first time that a Ramadan dinner had been held at the White House. A group of 50 ambassadors from Muslim countries attended. The President said, "I extend warm greetings to Muslims throughout the United States and around the world."

President George Bush marks the end of Ramadan by reading to Muslim children from Washington, D.C.

THE MESSAGE OF RAMADAN

For Muslims, Ramadan is a chance to renew their faith and spend time with loved ones. Ramadan is also a time to remember the poor and the hungry. Charity and good deeds allow Muslims to spread the Islamic message of peace and brotherhood.

GLOSSARY

Allah (AWL uh) — the supreme being of the Muslims

Eid al-Fitr (EE id ahl FIT uhr) — the first three days of Shawwal

Hibiscus (HIGH biss cuss) — a kind of tea

Iftar (IF tahr) — a meal taken at night during Ramadan

Islam (IZ lum) — a religion based on the teachings of the Qur'an

Kunafa (koo NAH fah) — a sweet pastry

mosque (MAWSK) — a Muslim house of worship

Mubarak (moo BAHR ack) — a word that means "blessed"

Muhammad (MOE ham mud) — the man who spread the teachings of Islam

Muslims (MUZZ lumz) — people who practice the Islam religion

Qur'an (kor ANN) — the Islam holy book

Sawm (SAHM) — fasting

Shawwal (SHAH wul) — the month after Ramadan

Tarawih (TARE ah wee) — a special prayer said at night during Ramadan

INDEX

Further Reading

Hoyt-Goldsmith, Diane. *Celebrating Ramadan*. Holiday House, 1998

Marchant, Kerena. *Id-Ul-Fitr*. Millbrook Press, 1998

Marchant, Kerena. *Muslim Festival Tales*. Raintree-Steck Vaughn, 2001

Websites To Visit

http://www.ifgstl.org/html/basics/ramadannf.htm

http://islam.about.com/cs/ramadan/

About The Author

Kieran Walsh is a writer of children's nonfiction books, primarily on historical and social studies topics. A graduate of Manhattan College, in Riverdale, NY, his degree is in Communications. Walsh has been involved in the children's book field as editor, proofreader, and illustrator as well as author.